ALAN GRATZ

RESIST
A STORY OF D-DAY

AN ORIGINAL STORY MADE JUST FOR YOU BY
SCHOLASTIC BOOK CLUBS

SCHOLASTIC INC.

Also by Alan Gratz

Allies
Grenade
Refugee
Projekt 1065
Prisoner B-3087
Code of Honor

Book ISBN 978-1-338-62180-8

10 9 8 7 6 5 4 3 2 1   19 20 21 22 23

Printed in the U.S.A. 40
First printing October 2019
Book design by Yaffa Jaskoll

NAZIS IN THE NIGHT

The door to the tavern down the street swung open, and Samira Zidane gasped in horror. Five Nazi officers staggered out into the lane, laughing and barking loudly at each other in German. Beside her, the little white dog that had become Samira's friend and companion in the last few hours, a scrappy terrier she'd named Cyrano, growled at the soldiers. He seemed to hate Nazis even more than Samira did.

The soldiers were too wrapped up in whatever they were laughing about to have spotted her yet, and Samira snatched Cyrano up in her arms and looked for a place to hide. It was long after curfew, the time the Nazis set for everyone in this part of occupied France to be inside their homes. People who were caught out after hours were often shot on sight as spies.

And Samira really *was* a spy. She had been helping her mother run messages to and from the French Resistance for months, and in the past few hours she'd actually helped the French Resistance sabotage German trains.

1

Samira's simple green dress and brown sweater might help her blend in as a villager if she was caught, but her light brown skin and black hair would definitely make her stand out. Samira was French-Algerian, and the Nazis would see she was one of the people they considered inferior and regularly shipped off to work camps.

Samira spotted a shop doorway that was set back from the street and hurried toward it, one hand around Cyrano and the other clutching the bottom of the blue kerchief she wore around her head. The one her mother had worn, before the Nazis had stolen her away. Quick and quiet as a fox, Samira jumped the two steps up to the doorway and darted into the small sliver of shadow where the Nazis wouldn't see her—and ran right into the other person who was already hiding there.

CABBAGE HEADS

Samira tried to back away, but the person she'd run into quickly put a hand on her arm to keep her still. As her eyes adjusted to the shadows, Samira saw who shared her hiding place. He was a boy with a pale, lean, hungry face and unkempt brown hair. Samira was twelve years old, and this boy couldn't have been more than three or four years older. He wore a torn brown jacket that was a size too big for him, a dirty white shirt, and gray pants that were held around his waist with a bit of rope.

The surprise of finding him here in the shadows had sent Samira's heart into her throat, but Cyrano had already decided he liked the boy and was licking his arm with enthusiasm.

The boy put a finger to his lips to tell Samira to be quiet, and she nodded. Whoever he was, he was as afraid of the Nazis as she was, and he didn't want to get caught either.

The German soldiers lingered in the street, still laughing and braying at each other. They had been out enjoying themselves at the local tavern, and now it was time for them to return to their beds in whatever garrison they were stationed in.

"Lousy cabbage heads," the boy whispered beside her. "Walking around like they own the place."

It was hard to argue they *didn't* own the place, Samira thought.

Nazi Germany had invaded France in 1940, and in no time at all they had rolled into Paris, the capital, and claimed the whole country for the German empire. The northern part of France, like here in Normandy, where Samira and her mother now lived, was under direct control of Germany, while the southern part of France was ruled by a French government that answered to the Nazis. For the last four years, Germany had moved soldiers and guns into barracks and fortresses all over France, solidifying their control. Now it was going to take a full-on Allied invasion—of soldiers from England and the United States—to drive them out again.

An invasion that was supposed to happen just a few hours from now!

Samira felt the boy tense beside her, and she looked back down the street. The Nazi soldiers were on the move again—and they were headed right for where Samira and the boy were hiding.

PEE BREAK

The Nazi soldiers swaggered down the street, conquerors enjoying their victory. They were getting closer. Closer. Samira and the boy were hidden in the shadows, but the doorway wasn't very deep. All it would take was for one of the soldiers to turn his head and see them, and it was all over. They would be captured and taken prisoner.

Will I be taken to where my mother is being held? Samira wondered. Her mother had been captured earlier that night, trying to help another French family escape a Nazi roundup. Samira thought her mother was being held with the others in a prison in the city of Bayeux. That's where Samira had been heading, hoping that the Germans would be too concerned with the Allied invasion to execute their prisoners at dawn, as they often did.

But what if the Allied invasion didn't work? What if the Germans shot down all the paratroopers and threw all the American and English soldiers and tanks coming up from the beaches back into the sea? Then her mother and all the other French prisoners would die. And if Samira was caught here and now, she'd be shot with them.

The German soldiers sang at the top of their lungs as they came closer, daring anyone to tell them to be quiet. No one would, of course. Every door in the little French village was shut and locked and every window shade pulled down tight while people quaked under their bed covers. The Nazis were real-life boogeymen. Sober, they were fearsome masters. Drunk, like these men were, they could become monsters.

Samira's breath caught as one of the soldiers broke away from the rest of the group and staggered toward the doorway where she and the boy were hiding. The soldier fumbled with his belt, and with dread, Samira realized he was coming this way to relieve himself.

Samira turned and tried the door handle to the shop, but it was closed. There was nowhere for her and the boy to go. They were trapped, and the Nazi was almost on top of them.

Beside her, the boy pulled a pistol from the waist of his pants. Samira's eyes went wide. She hadn't noticed the gun before. The boy looked at her with wild eyes, as if telling her he would kill the Nazi soldier rather than be caught. Samira panicked. Being captured by the Nazis was one thing—*shooting one*, that would turn the drunk soldiers into monsters for sure. Each of the Germans carried a pistol of his own at his side, and if they heard a single shot and saw their comrade fall they would fire every last bullet they had into the shadows of this doorway. The boy couldn't shoot them all. Samira and Cyrano and the boy would probably be dead before he could fire a second shot.

Samira's mind raced. What to do—what to do? The German soldier was going to see them any second now. The boy raised his pistol. Cyrano growled.

A calm came over Samira. The same kind of calm she felt before she walked out onto the stage during a play at school. When all the rehearsing, all the memorization of lines, all the butterflies suddenly went away, and she stepped out of herself and into another character. Became someone else. She felt that same liberation of spirit now, and in that moment, she knew what she had to do.

Samira put Cyrano on the ground, pretended to pull the door closed behind her, and stepped out into the street.

ON STAGE

"*No,*" the boy whispered, reaching out for her at the last second. But he was too late. Samira stepped out into the light of the full moon, drawing her kerchief close and hugging an arm to her chest against the cold.

"Go potty now, Cyrano. Hurry," she said. Then she looked up and saw the German soldier right in front of her. She sucked in her breath and stopped, acting surprised, as if this was the first time she'd seen him.

Samira appearing out of the shadows so suddenly in the middle of the night startled the German soldier, and he staggered back. Cyrano ran circles around the Nazi, yipping at him, and now Samira had the attention of all the drunk soldiers in the street.

One of the soldiers asked her in German what she was doing outside so late after curfew.

"I'm sorry," Samira replied in French. "I don't speak German." Which wasn't true. She spoke a little, the same way everybody else in German-occupied France had picked up a little German. But she wasn't going to tell them that.

The German soldier groaned and repeated himself in French. "Why are you out after curfew?"

"My dog was scratching at the door like he had to pee," Samira told them.

"So I see," said one of the other soldiers. He pointed at Cyrano, who was, at that moment, peeing on the leg of the German soldier who'd been headed off into the doorway to do the same thing.

"Hey! Cut that out!" the soldier said, hopping backward.

His friends fell all over themselves laughing.

"I'm sorry! I'm so sorry," Samira said, running after Cyrano. The dog led her on a merry chase among the Nazis, nipping at them as he went.

"Your dog doesn't seem to like Germans," another soldier said.

"No, no," Samira said. "He loves you."

Cyrano put the lie to her words by biting at the heels of the soldier who had to pee. Samira scooped up Cyrano in her arms and hid a smile.

High up in the sky behind the soldiers, Samira saw the black silhouettes of half a dozen parachutes against the bright full moon. *The invasion.* Soon these German soldiers would have lots more to worry about, but for now, Samira had to save herself and the boy in the doorway.

"All right. Your dog's done his business," said a soldier holding a wine bottle. He seemed to be the one in charge. "Now go on back to bed. We'll forgive you being out after curfew this one time, but next time he pees on the rug instead. Understand?"

"Yes, yes. Thank you," Samira said. She looked back and forth between the doorway and the soldiers. A few more steps and they would see the boy.

"Are you headed back to the garrison?" Samira asked.

The soldier with the bottle narrowed his eyes warily.

"Why?" he asked.

"Because the garrison isn't that way, it's *that* way," Samira said, pointing in the other direction down the street. Samira had no idea where their fort was in this part of France. Her adventures before now had taken her far from home tonight. But she hoped the German soldiers were too drunk to know one direction from another.

The soldiers looked back and forth and frowned, and their leader cursed.

"These French villages all look alike," he said in German. He shook his head and started off down the road in the other direction, and the soldiers followed him.

"*Au revoir!*" Samira called to the soldiers as she went back into the shadows to join the boy. She worried that was laying it on a bit thick, but the soldiers walked on without looking back.

"That was amazing," the boy whispered when the soldiers were out of sight. "I can't believe you did that."

"I can't believe you were going to shoot him!" Samira said.

The boy blushed and put the pistol away.

"My name is Lucien," he told her as they stepped out from the shadows.

"I'm Atalanta," Samira told him. "And this is Cyrano," she said, holding up the dog. "Those are our code names. We work for the French Resistance."

"I'm with the Resistance too!" Lucien told her. "My code name is Lycastus."

"Then come help me find my mother!" Samira said. "She's being held in Bayeux."

INDEPENDENCE

"Come with you to Bayeux? But that's hours from here! I can't," Lucien said. "Besides, I have a mission." He pulled a pair of wire cutters from his pocket. "I have to cut all the telephone lines from here to Saint-Georges so the cabbage heads can't call for reinforcements." He leaned in conspiratorially. "The invasion is happening tonight!"

"I know," Samira said. "My mother was captured delivering the message to the fighters in the woods. If the English and the Americans make it up off the beach in time, the Germans might not shoot her at dawn with the other prisoners. But if the invasion isn't successful—"

"It will be!" Lucien told her. "It has to be!" He turned to leave. "You better get out of here before those soldiers realize you sent them off in the wrong direction. And stay off the roads if you can!"

"Wait!" Samira called, but the boy was already running away into the darkness.

"Looks like it's just you and me again, Cyrano," Samira told the little dog. She let him down, and he shook himself and fell into a trot alongside her.

Cyrano's family had been taken as prisoners at the same time Samira's mother had, and it seemed like he and Samira were the only ones interested in saving their lives. But Bayeux was the biggest city in this part of Normandy, and a great many Nazi soldiers were stationed there. There was no way she and Cyrano could free the other prisoners on their own. Samira was determined to get to Bayeux by morning nonetheless, to be there when the Allies arrived. And if they didn't . . .

Samira felt a pang in her chest at the thought. But everything in its own time, as her mother would say. No sense crying before you were hurt.

Samira left the road, as Lucien had advised, stepping carefully through cow pastures. But always north, toward Bayeux. Tall hedgerows hid her from view. Overhead, airplanes droned by constantly, accompanied by the *boom-boom-boom* of German anti-aircraft guns. Gray clouds came and went, but in the light from the moon and the tracer fire she could still see the tiny black dots that filled the skies like the speckles on Normandy's cows. Allied paratroopers, dropping behind enemy lines to fight the Germans. Her heart swelled at the idea.

We will finally be free from the Nazis, she thought. After four long years of living in fear, it was almost too much to hope for. What would she and her mother do then? she wondered. A little voice inside her said, *"Your mother's not free yet. Might never be free. Might be—"*

No. She quashed the thought and let herself dream. She had to live with hope, not fear, or she would curl up into a ball and cry right here in the meadow with the cows.

When the war was over, she and her mother would return to Paris. Yes. Her mother would go back to the university and study law, like before, and then they would travel to Algeria, in North

Africa. The French colony that Samira called her own but had never been to. Never seen. The French would grant Algeria their independence for helping free France from German rule, and Samira and her mother would no longer be second-class citizens. They and all the other Algerians would rise from the ashes of this world war and build a new, free nation.

The sound of gunshots filled the air, and Samira ducked instinctively. Fighting? Here? Now? But she was hours from the coast! The sounds of war were getting closer, but everywhere she looked, she saw only sleepy cows and open fields. There—in the sky—a paratrooper was coming down just a few hundred kilometers away! All the other parachutes had looked like little mushrooms in the clouds, but this one was as big as a tree, and the dark silhouette of a man dangled from the bottom. *The Germans must be shooting at him*, Samira thought. She didn't see any German soldiers, but the field was filled with the sound of gunfire.

The man on the parachute swung down, down, down, until he crashed into a stand of trees at the far end of the field. Samira could still hear gunshots and explosions, but she had to find the man. He might need her help.

And maybe, just maybe, he could help Samira free her mother.

DEAD OR ALIVE

Cyrano yipped merrily, his little paws a blur as he ran alongside Samira. The sound of the gunfire and explosions grew louder, and Samira ducked again, worried she might be shot. But she didn't see any soldiers, didn't *see* any explosions. She and Cyrano made it to the small cluster of trees, and she slowed. This was where she had seen the parachute come down, and she fought to calm her pounding heart as she searched the ground for the soldier.

Nothing. Nothing. The sound of battle filled the small wood all around her, but she and Cyrano were totally alone. The trees—the paratrooper must have gotten caught in the trees!

Samira looked up, and immediately she saw him. The soldier's parachute had gotten caught in the branches of an oak tree, and he was hanging loose in the wind. He was no more than a silhouette, and his arms and legs dangled limply from his body.

"Hello?" Samira called out. She looked around, worried that any German soldiers in the area might have heard her, then tried again. "Hello?"

She was speaking French, and she assumed the paratrooper spoke English—he was likely from the United States or the United Kingdom, after all—but he didn't say anything back in any language. Had his landing knocked him unconscious? Had the Nazis shot him on the way down, and he was dead? Samira had to know. Had to help, if she could.

"Wait here," she told Cyrano, and she began to climb.

It was hard to get started. The oak's lowest branch was almost out of her reach, and when she grabbed it, it was almost too thin and weak to support her. But Samira was small and deft, and she scrabbled up until she found a thicker branch to hold her. Up and up she climbed. It seemed to take forever, and all the while anti-aircraft guns boomed overhead and the gunshots and mortar explosions continued. Below her, Cyrano got smaller and smaller, but the paratrooper was looking bigger. And, unfortunately, less alive. He hung lifelessly, like a dummy stuffed with straw. Samira's breaths came short and quick, and she felt tears well up in her eyes. What would she do if he really was dead?

Samira moved around the backside of the trunk to climb up onto a higher branch, and when she came around again, she would be face-to-face with the soldier. She closed her eyes, took a deep breath, and shinnied carefully around to the other side.

He has to be alive. He has *to be alive*, she told herself, and she opened her eyes.

Samira's heart stopped. The soldier wasn't alive. But he wasn't dead either.

The paratrooper was a dummy.

RUPERT

Samira blinked in surprise. She hadn't been imagining things when she'd thought of the man hanging from his parachute cords as a dummy filled with straw. That's exactly what he was! The dummy wore an imitation of a soldier's uniform, complete with helmet and boots. But underneath, "he" was only rough burlap cloth that had been hastily sewn and stuffed in the shape of a person. A very small person. From the ground, the dummy had looked like a regular-sized human being! It must have been a trick of perspective, because up close the dummy didn't look much like a man at all. Its head was pear-shaped, its chest was a rectangle, and its arms and legs were perfectly straight and disproportioned.

Stenciled on his burlap chest was the name RUPERT.

"Aren't you a little short for a paratrooper?" Samira asked.

Rupert didn't answer, of course. But he did make a noise. Now that Samira was up close, she understood that *this* was where the sounds of the battle were coming from. There was a tiny speaker inside Rupert, playing a recording of gunshots and mortar explosions! Samira smiled. What a clever trick, to drop dummies over Normandy and make the Nazis run all over the place trying to fight Allied soldiers who weren't there.

Samira's stomach suddenly tied itself into a knot. If the Allied paratroopers weren't real—if this was all a trick—did that mean the Allies *weren't* really invading France tonight? Or that they were invading somewhere else? Farther to the north, where France was closer to England? Or farther south, where the German defenses were weaker? Samira's arms and legs went limp, and she had to hug the tree trunk not to fall.

If the Allies weren't really invading this part of Normandy, the Nazis in Bayeux wouldn't be distracted in the morning, and her mother and all the other prisoners would be shot at dawn.

The reality of it sank in, and Samira felt herself tearing up again. All night long, ever since her mother had been captured by the Nazis, she had pinned her hopes for her mother's rescue on the Allied soldiers coming up from the beaches and dropping from planes. But if the invasion here was nothing more than a bunch of dummies, meant to draw the Germans' attention away from the real invasion happening somewhere else—no one was coming to save Samira's mother.

Which meant she was going to have to do it herself.

Samira wiped the tears from her eyes and got down to business. Rupert might not be a real soldier, but he could still help Samira with her mission. That helmet would fit, and so would those boots. And that recording inside him—a recording of gunshots and explosions—could be very helpful if she could somehow remove the device and take it with her.

Keeping one arm wrapped around the tree trunk, Samira began to loosen Rupert's uniform. The dummy kept spinning on his cords and swinging away from her, and when she reached out to grab hold of him again she yanked down too hard. The parachute tangled up in the branches above her tore with a sound like ripping paper, and suddenly Rupert went tumbling down through the branches. Samira watched him fall like the rag doll he was, and Cyrano ran away in fear of the plummeting thing.

Then the dummy hit the ground and—*Ka-KOOM*. It exploded into a ball of fire!

BE BRAVE

"Cyrano!" Samira cried.

Her first thought was for her loyal companion, but a moment later Cyrano danced back into view, barking angrily at the dummy for exploding and scaring him like that. Relieved, Samira hastily climbed back down the tree, black smoke and the smell of burning burlap filling her nose. To avoid Rupert's fiery remains, she leaped down from higher up than she would have liked. She landed in a heap and scuffed her knee in the fall.

Cyrano ran over to welcome her back, then was off to bark at the burning dummy again.

Samira hobbled over to see that Rupert was almost gone. There hadn't been much of him to begin with, and now there was just a charred spot on the ground where he'd landed. Even his helmet and boots, Samira realized, had been made out of papier-mâché. The whole thing had been designed to explode and burn, leaving almost no trace of what it had been. The recording that had been inside was nothing more than a few burnt wires and a melted battery. Rupert wasn't going to be any help to her after all.

Worse, the explosion had alerted some German soldiers nearby. Samira could hear them calling out to each other, saw their electric torches flashing across the field. It was time for her and Cyrano to exit stage left, and fast. She snatched up the little dog and ran. Away from the Nazis. Toward Bayeux and her mother.

Samira was tired. So tired. She just wanted to be a kid again. Just wanted to go to school and have normal problems, like homework and tests and girls who teased her. But this was her life now, and she had to be brave. Braver than she had ever been before. Brave like her mother.

Samira thought about her mother as she ducked and ran and slipped through the fields and hedgerows. Her mother had been brave enough to leave her home in Algeria and come here to France, before the war, to study law. How many women did that? And then, when the war started and the Nazis rolled into Paris, Samira's mom had to be brave again. Her husband, Samira's father, was killed in the streets protesting the Nazis. That awful night, while seven-year-old Samira had wanted to do nothing more than bury her head under her pillow and cry, Kenza Zidane had bundled up her daughter, thrown everything they could take with them in a knapsack, and carried them both away into the night. Carried her daughter and everything they owned through towns and fields and villages, hiding out from the Nazis all the way, until they found refuge here in Normandy among friends from the university.

Then, almost immediately, Samira's mother began working for the French Resistance. Mostly she had run messages to and from the Resistance fighters hiding out in the woods at night, taking Samira along with her under the pretense of taking her sick daughter to the doctor. But more than once they had been asked to house downed Allied bomber pilots working their way back north to cross the Channel to England. If the German army had ever found any of the

Allied soldiers hiding in Samira's house, she and her mother would both have been killed by the Nazis.

It was a risk Samira's mother had never questioned.

Kenza Zidane was the bravest person Samira knew. And now Samira had to rely on *her* own bravery to save her mother's life, the way her mother had saved so many others.

Behind the dark field where Samira walked, something cracked and crashed, making her jump.

Samira spun around. Exploding through the tops of the trees, coming in for a landing right on top of her, was an Allied airplane!

CRASH LANDING

Samira threw herself out of the way as the airplane whooshed by overhead. It hit the ground with a sickening crunch, bouncing once, twice, and then flipping straight up into the air, tail first, as the front end carved up the earth. *Crash! Crack! Smash!* It was so loud the whole of France had to hear it. The plane slammed back down flat on the ground but kept moving. Samira covered her ears as the thing slid, twisted, and skidded toward the hedgerow at the end of the clearing, and then—*wham!* The plane hit a tree and stopped dead in its tracks.

Samira peeked up from where she lay on the ground, and Cyrano trotted up beside her nervously. Was it an Allied bomber the Nazis had shot down? Samira braced for the explosion. If it was a bomber, it would be filled with bombs, after all. And even if it had dumped all its bombs, it would have tanks full of petrol to run its engines. Samira held her breath, waiting.

One of the plane's wings snapped off and fell to the ground, and Samira jumped. But nothing went boom.

Had the crew survived the landing? Just the day before, they might have needed the help of the Resistance to find an escape route from German-occupied France. Today, Invasion Day, it was Samira who needed *their* help.

If they were alive.

Samira pulled herself up and approached the plane cautiously. She was still afraid it was going to blow up. Worse, it didn't have the usual markings of an Allied airplane. Was it a German plane? The Germans didn't have many planes left, but it *could* be. But it didn't *look* like a regular airplane either. It was small and boxy, and as Samira got closer, she was stunned to see that the wing that had broken off was made of wood and canvas. The whole *thing* was made of wood and canvas. It didn't have any propellers either.

It was a glider, not an airplane. But what was it doing here? Now? And where was the crew? Why hadn't anyone come out of it? Samira crept up to the open door on the side of the glider and peeked inside. It was dark, but she could make out a couple dozen shapes. More dummies! They sat slumped over in their seats, helmets lolling to the side.

Samira's heart sank all over again. She couldn't believe it. She understood making the Nazis chase dummies dropped by parachutes. But what was the point of crash-landing a plane full of Ruperts?

Unless they were all going to explode!

Samira drew back from the doorway. She had to get out of here! But where was Cyrano?

Yip! Yip-yip!

Cyrano was inside the plane! He was running up and down the aisle of the glider, barking at the dummies.

"Cyrano! Cyrano, come out of there!" Samira cried. "It's going to blow up!"

But Cyrano wasn't coming out. Samira was going to have go in and get him.

Samira took a step inside the glider, and it creaked and groaned. Cyrano was hopping around at the back of the plane, yipping at the dummies. Samira couldn't reach him. Not without going farther down the aisle. She turned sideways, trying to slide by the Ruperts, but there wasn't enough room for her. She brushed up against one of the dummies and it slid toward her in its seat. She yipped louder than Cyrano as she jumped back, and the dummy groaned.

Groaned?

Samira looked closer. It wasn't a dummy after all. None of them were.

The glider was filled with unconscious soldiers!

WOLVES

Samira poked the groaning man, gently but firmly. He shook his head and moaned. All around Samira, more of the "dummies" came to life, rubbing their faces and cracking their necks. Cyrano yipped happily, and one of the soldiers shushed him. They must all have been knocked unconscious by the crash, and they were all just now coming to.

A soldier at the front slapped himself awake and unhooked himself from his seat. He was short, but he held himself with such authority that Samira was sure he was the leader. He had pale skin, wide shoulders, and a bald head underneath his crooked helmet. He straightened his helmet, whispered urgently in English to the other soldiers, then asked Samira a question she didn't understand. She didn't speak English, and she said so. In French.

"Major Hughes wants to know who you are, and how long we've been out," another soldier near her said in badly accented French. He was a young white man with black hair and glasses.

"Oh! My name is Samira," she told the soldier. In her surprise, she had forgotten to use her code name, but it hardly seemed to matter now. "And you just crashed a few minutes ago. You almost landed on me."

The soldier reported what she had said to the major at the front of the plane, and Major Hughes whispered again to his soldiers, urging them out of the plane. Samira was suddenly caught up in a flurry of soldiers collecting their weapons and trying to climb out of the glider.

"Pardon us, miss, but we've got to get moving," the soldier who spoke French said. "If you and your dog could get out of the way?"

Samira grabbed Cyrano and slipped back out of the glider. The soldiers quickly followed, still cracking their necks and blinking, trying to wake themselves up.

"Where are you from? Are you here for the invasion?" Samira asked the soldier who spoke French.

"We came from England. My name's Clarke," he replied. "And yes, we're part of the invasion. Now run along. We've got a bridge to capture."

"The bridge over the Seulles? That's just down the road!" Samira said. "I can take you there!"

"You know where it is?" Clarke asked.

Samira did. Clarke told the major, and Hughes agreed to have Samira show them the way. Samira was delighted. Not only did this mean the invasion *was* happening, here and now in Normandy, but if the English soldiers were going to take the bridge over the Seulles River, that meant they were headed north too—the same direction Samira was going. That meant they were marching toward Bayeux, where her mother and the other prisoners were being held. There was a chance her mother would be saved by dawn after all!

Samira waved for Clarke and the other soldiers to follow her. There was no time to waste! They looked a frightful sight, Samira thought as they snuck through the small wood. Twenty-some-odd camouflaged soldiers, each carrying machine guns at their hips and grenades on their belts. All of them had shoe black on their faces—all but the two black soldiers—to blend in with the shadows. They moved as one, skulking silently through the woods like a pack of wolves stalking their prey. Never a misstep. Never a moment's hesitation. Samira shivered. She was glad they were on her side.

They came to the edge of the wood, and Samira pointed. Just ahead of them was the bridge they had been sent to take. Samira and her mother had avoided this water-crossing on their way south to pass along the news of the invasion to the French Resistance. It was a steel-girder bridge—bigger and newer than most in Normandy—and its metal trestles loomed big and dark above them. To one side of the road, the Nazis had built a concrete turret to house an anti-tank gun, and Samira could see two figures—Nazi guards—walking the length of the bridge.

Pakow!

A rifle shot made Samira jump, and one of the German guards on the bridge crumpled and fell. The English were already attacking!

"Go! Go! Go!" Major Hughes yelled, and suddenly Samira was in the middle of a battle.

THE BATTLE OF THE BRIDGE

Bang! Bang! Tut-tut-tut-tut-tut.

Samira dropped to the ground and pulled Cyrano close as bullets flew. The English soldiers thundered up onto the steel bridge, their boots ringing like a hailstorm on a tin roof. The second German guard fired a flare gun in the air, and it lit up the scene for Samira. She watched as Clarke, the soldier who'd spoken to her in French, cut the second German sentry down with his machine gun.

English soldiers threw grenades into the pillbox and—*POOM. POOM-POOM. PaKOOM!*—it exploded in a cloud of concrete dust and flames. The Germans who weren't on guard duty were awake now, and rifles barked on both sides, but the English soldiers swarmed the bridge and the adjoining bunker. Samira saw a German guard shoot another sun-bright flare into the dark sky, then turn tail and run.

German machine gunners peppered the attackers, and bullets pinged off the metal struts of the bridge. Samira saw Clarke rush the sandbagged trench where the German gunners were hiding and fire a burst with his own machine gun. Another grenade took care of the rest of the German soldiers in the trench with a *POOM*.

There was a second pillbox at the other end of the bridge. Samira heard its big gun fire—*paKOW*—but it didn't hit anyone. It was made to hit tanks, not men, and all it did was blast a crater in the grass a hundred meters away. Samira lost sight of Clarke, but she saw another English soldier fire a shoulder cannon at the pillbox right before he was hit by a German bullet and went down. The missile he'd fired was right on target though, and the second pillbox exploded in a gust of fire and smoke.

From the sound of things, there was another machine gun nest on the other side of the bridge. Samira heard the *POOM-POOM-POOM* of grenades, and the heavy machine gun fire stopped.

And then, as quickly as it had begun, the battle was over. The bridge belonged to the English. The first attack of the invasion Samira had been witness to was a success!

Samira waited a few minutes after the last of the gunshots had been fired. Then she let Cyrano go and carefully made her way over to the bridge. Cyrano ran from place to place along the bridge, sniffing and investigating.

The pillboxes were still smoking, and there were scorch marks all over the metal girders. A few of the English soldiers had been wounded, and Samira saw a medic bandaging them up. The only man who had died was the one Samira had seen fire the shoulder cannon that took out the second pillbox.

There were still German bunkers with soldiers hiding in them, apparently, and the major dispatched soldiers to clear the trenches with phosphorous grenades. Major Hughes stopped briefly to mourn the man who had died, then was just as quickly talking into a radio telephone connected to a pack on another soldier's chest.

But where was Clarke? Samira needed to talk to him—needed to tell them all to get moving on to Bayeux!

OBEYING ORDERS

Samira found Clarke being treated by a medic. Her heart skipped a beat, worried he might be mortally injured, but he had only taken a bullet to his arm. He would live to fight another day.

"Thanks for the directions," Clarke told her. "But you really shouldn't be here. The Germans might have rigged the bridge to explode."

Samira's eyes went wide, but Clarke was quick to calm her.

"Don't worry. If they were going to do it, they would have done it. Our engineers are searching for explosives now. If they find anything, they'll disable them."

Samira breathed a sigh of relief. These soldiers were very good at their jobs. If all the Allies fought like this, the invasion would be over in no time.

"Bayeux isn't far from here," Samira told him. "Just another three hours or so up the road. We can be there before dawn if we hurry!"

"I'm afraid we're not going anywhere, miss. Not any time soon," Clarke said. "Our mission was to take this bridge and hold it until the soldiers come up from the beach—or until the Germans come try to take it back from us. We're not going to Bayeux. Not today."

"What? No!" Samira said. But once Clarke said it, she realized that the soldiers were settling in. Taking up defensive positions in the very same bunkers and trenches they had just cleared. "But you *have* to push on to Bayeux!" Samira told Clarke. "My mother is being held prisoner there by the Nazis!"

Clarke looked genuinely apologetic. "Sorry, miss. We have a job to do. Your mother will be okay though. I'm sure of it."

Samira's disappointment burst into a flame of anger inside her. How could he know her mother was going to be all right? Clarke hadn't lived here in Normandy for the past four years. None of them had. They hadn't seen the way the Nazis treated the French people here. What they did to their prisoners. He didn't understand.

"Please," Samira begged. "If you could just talk to the major."

Clarke grimaced. "Oh, I couldn't do that, miss. I'm sorry. It's not my place to question orders. But there's soldiers landing all over Normandy right this very minute. Maybe some of them are attacking Bayeux. And in any case, the boys coming off the boats'll be up off the beaches before too long."

But not soon enough, thought Samira. *Not soon enough for my mother and all the other prisoners.*

"Then I'll go do it myself," Samira said with more anger than she meant to, and she turned to leave.

Clarke put out a hand to stop her. "Wait. How long has it been since you ate something? Here." He pulled a cardboard box of biscuits out of his pack and gave it to her.

"I'm not hungry," Samira said. It was a lie. Samira was starving. She hadn't eaten for hours, and then it had only been potatoes. Again. But she didn't want food from Clarke, she wanted his help freeing her mother. Accepting anything else seemed like giving up.

"For your dog, then," Clarke said. "He looks hungry."

Cyrano had returned from his investigations and was standing on his hind legs, trying desperately to sniff at the food in the box.

"For Cyrano, then," Samira said, and the gnawing ache in her stomach subsided a bit, knowing she would give in and eat some of the biscuits soon.

"There's water too," Clarke said. "Drink some before you go. You should stay here with us, but if you're going to be roaming around Normandy all by yourself tonight, you should have this."

Clarke unhooked a leather scabbard from his belt and handed it over. Samira gripped the handle and pulled out a dagger with a blade as long as her hand. She gasped.

"Be careful, miss," Clarke said. "It's sharp. Hopefully you won't have to use that on anybody, but just in case. And I'm sorry we can't come with you. If everybody did what they wanted and disobeyed their orders, the whole invasion would fall apart."

Samira softened. She wished it were otherwise—these soldiers could rout the Nazis in Bayeux in no time!—but she understood. Maybe she could find some soldiers whose mission was to take Bayeux. Maybe Allied soldiers were attacking the city right now! The only way to know was to get there as soon as she could.

EXHAUSTED

Samira had been walking for hours. It was almost dawn—that strange time when it's still dark but the birds wake up and the forest comes to life with the scuttling of little animals. The air was sharp and cool, and dew glistened on the grass. Any minute now, the sun would peek up over the horizon, turning the blue-gray sky orange.

And Samira would be too late.

She was weary, but hope, fear, worry kept her moving. The biscuits Clarke had given her were long since eaten, shared with Cyrano, of course. Now Samira carried her companion, his little legs too tired to walk another meter. His head rested on Samira's arm like she was his own personal pillow, and she could feel the rise and fall of his tiny chest as he dozed.

Samira had left the fields and was walking along the road now. It was dangerous, but it was the best way to know she was headed in the right direction. Besides, the Germans had flooded most of the pastures close to the city, hoping to catch Allied paratroopers. She had seen more of those coming down in the night, but not so many now. And no more gliders. Was that all the Allies were sending? And where were all the ones she'd seen coming down through the night? What missions did they have? Were any of them attacking Bayeux?

Or was that the job of the soldiers coming up off the beaches, like Clarke had said?

What will I do if the soldiers are too late? Samira wondered. She had Clarke's dagger now, but what good was a girl with a dagger against an entire German garrison? And what if she didn't even get the chance to fight? What if her mother and the other prisoners were shot before she even got there?

Samira stumbled and dropped to her knees on the pavement, doing her best not to fall over on Cyrano. Her scraped knee screamed in pain, and she cried out softly. She was exhausted. She couldn't remember the last time she had stayed up all night long. Had she ever? She was so tired it was hard to think. She wanted to lie down. Close her eyes. Just rest for a few minutes. But she knew that if she did, she wouldn't get up again. Not in time to save her mother.

A bright light appeared in the road ahead of her, and Samira squinted. The purr of an engine reached her, and she clambered to her feet. Someone was coming!

PAKOW

Samira staggered off the road just as a motorcycle buzzed by, going so fast in the gray predawn that she couldn't even see if it was German or otherwise. She was just wondering if the motorcyclist had spotted her when another light broke down the road. And another. And another. And then suddenly there was a thunder of engines, and a herd of motorcycles roared past her. Cyrano was wide awake now, and he barked furiously at the rumbling things as they passed, his protests drowned out in the noise. Samira held on to him as he wiggled. Who were they? And where were they going in such a hurry?

Samira watched, dazed, as the motorcycles were followed by truck after truck of soldiers. Some of the trucks had no covers on the backs, and she could see the soldiers sitting side by side on long benches, facing one another, rifles between their legs. Other trucks were covered with canvas tops, and she could see the soldiers inside when they passed.

German soldiers.

Samira blinked in wonder at the never-ending procession. Troop transports. Motorcycles. Field cars. Half-tracks—that strange combination of truck and tank with rubber wheels in the front and treads in the back. And then *actual* tanks. At least a dozen of them, clanking by in slow motion, belching exhaust. Samira didn't know how long she'd stood there gaping before she realized she should hide. Take cover somewhere. Her mind flashed to the scabbard she'd tied to her belt, the knife Clarke had given her. She could defend herself, if she had to.

But no one seemed to care about her. They all saw Samira—the truck drivers and infantrymen and tank crews and officers. They all saw her, out after curfew, and not one of them stopped, and not one of them said anything. It was like Samira didn't matter anymore. They had something bigger to worry about now, and no one had time for a girl and her dog. Samira remembered just a few hours ago, when she and the boy from the French Resistance had been so worried about being caught in the street. But that was before the Allies had dropped thousands of soldiers on Normandy. Before the invasion had really begun. Now she might as well have been a rock for all any of them cared.

One of the soldiers manning a mounted machine gun in the back of a half-track noticed her at last. He aimed his big machine gun at her and tracked her through its sights. Samira sucked in her breath, suddenly regretting that she hadn't run and hidden when she had a chance. It was too late now, and if she moved, he would only gun her down for sport.

Samira held her breath and looked right back at the soldier. She couldn't see his eyes, but she knew he could see her looking at him, could tell from the way the barrel of his machine gun stayed on her that he was still watching her as the half-track drove past.

Pakow. Samira could see the soldier's mouth silently form the word as he pretended to shoot her. He didn't pull the trigger though. Not for real. As the half-track drove out of range, he stood and rested his arms on the top of the gun, smirking at her like a tiger who had let a mouse go by.

And then they were gone. The last of the trucks rumbled down the road, and everything was still and quiet again. Samira trembled but stayed on her feet. She put Cyrano down, and he ran out into the road to sniff at all the new smells the trucks had left in their wake. Samira couldn't believe it. It felt like the entire German army had passed them by. That wasn't all of them, she knew, but it was more soldiers, more trucks, more tanks than Samira had ever seen in one place. Were they headed for Major Hughes and his team at the bridge? Or were they going somewhere else? Wherever it was, she was sure it was because of the Allied invasion.

Today's Allied invasion. With a start, Samira realized that while she'd been mesmerized by the German army driving by, the sun had come up. It was officially morning, and the Germans shot their prisoners at dawn.

Samira ran.

AN EMPTY NEST

The city of Bayeux was still asleep—or in hiding—as Samira ran through its streets. Ever since the Nazi occupation began, it was always safer inside your home than out. But something was wrong. More wrong than usual, even during the occupation. What should have been a bustling, living city was quietly hibernating. It was eerie.

The lights were off in the bakeries. Cafe chairs were stacked on their tables. The druggists were closed. White lilies filled the buckets in a florist's shop window, but no one was there to sell them. Blinds on windows were drawn, and shutters were closed. When the Bayeux cathedral's bells chimed seven o'clock in the morning, Samira started at the sound. Up and down the narrow cobblestone streets, not a soul was out and about.

That's when Samira realized what else was missing: the Nazis. For four years, they had been an ever-present menace everywhere you went. Nazi soldiers on street corners. In village pubs. In shops and restaurants, on bridges and trains. You couldn't turn around without running into a German soldier. But here in Bayeux, they were all gone. She hadn't seen a single Nazi soldier since a parade of them had driven by her a half hour ago. Were they hiding too?

No—the parade she had seen *was* Bayeux's Germans! She didn't see any soldiers here in the city because they had all just driven past her. The Nazis had abandoned Bayeux! Whether they were going to attack Allied soldiers somewhere else or defend some other larger city, she didn't know. But it didn't matter! All that mattered was that her mother and the other prisoners might not be dead!

But where were they?

"Cyrano, we have to find our families," Samira told her little companion. Cyrano was trotting from sidewalk to sidewalk, sniffing at things and lifting his leg here and there to mark where he'd been. She wished he understood her urgency. Just because the Nazis had retreated, that didn't mean her mother and the others were safe. The Nazis were like wasps. Even if you thought they were ignoring you, one of them could still sting you when you were least expecting it.

If anyone would know where her mother and the prisoners were being held, it would be one of the people of the city. But where *were* they? There was only one way to find out.

Samira ran up to the first door that looked like someone's home and knocked.

THEY ALWAYS COME BACK

"Hello?" Samira called. "Is anyone there?"

She saw a curtain rustle in the window, but no one answered the door.

"I'm looking for my mother. She's with other prisoners, brought here to the city overnight," Samira called through the door.

Still no answer.

She went to the next door and tried again. Nothing. There were people behind these doors. She was sure of it. But they were too scared to answer.

"Look! The Nazis are gone!" Samira called out. "I saw them! They're headed south and east. It's the invasion! It's beginning!"

"Go away," someone called from an upstairs window. Samira spun, but she couldn't see who or where they were. "They can still come back. They always come back."

"No, you don't understand!" Samira called. "I just need to find out where my mother was taken!"

Cyrano yipped, joining in on the conversation, but as the sound of his bark echoed away, the city became silent again. Everyone was scared. No one knew what was coming next, and not knowing was the worst part. Would they be freed by the Allies? Or would the invasion fail, and the Nazis come back stronger, meaner, and angrier than before?

Samira understood their fear. But she was frustrated too. She was so tired. So very, very tired. She had worked so hard to help the Resistance, to help the Allied soldiers, to hike back and forth across Normandy on foot to get here just after dawn. And now the Nazis were gone and her mother might be somewhere close by, but no one would help.

"*Please,*" Samira begged. She couldn't keep the tears out of her voice. Cyrano came up alongside her and whimpered, sharing her sadness, and Samira slumped.

"Girl, come here," someone whispered. It was an elderly white woman with a faded red kerchief tied around her head. She had opened her door just a crack a few houses down and was peeking outside.

Samira dried her eyes and ran toward the house. Cyrano was faster, and when he tried to run inside the woman closed the door even more, making the space too small for him to fit. Samira's heart skipped a beat—she didn't want the old woman to close her door again just because of Cyrano! Samira snatched up the little dog and waited hopefully.

The old woman opened the door again and took a quick look up and down the street.

"The old hotel, across from the cathedral," the woman whispered. "That's where they take the prisoners they bring in from the countryside. If your mother is still alive, that's where she'll be."

A hotel across from the cathedral! Samira didn't know the city, but the cathedral was easy enough to see. Its twin spires stood tall over the rooftops in the distance.

"Thank you! Thank you!" Samira cried as she ran. Maybe her mother was still alive. Maybe there was still time . . .

"Good luck, girl," the old woman called after her. "Maybe the cabbage heads really are gone for good!"

LEFT BEHIND

Samira turned the last corner to the town square, where the cathedral stood. It was a huge brown and gray building, ancient and imposing. It had gargoyles for rainspouts, and arches to hold up its walls, and the whole front of it was covered with beautiful, intricate, stained-glass windows that had somehow survived the Allied bombing of Normandy, just like the rest of the city. *Somebody up there must like Bayeux*, Samira thought. Somebody up in those bombers.

Another day, Samira would have stopped and stared. But not today. Today she only had eyes for the humble building across the street from the cathedral, an old hotel the Nazis had turned into their headquarters.

As she ran down the street, the front door of the hotel opened, and out walked the first person Samira had seen on the street that whole morning:

A Nazi soldier with a rifle over his shoulder.

Samira slid to a stop, turned, and ran for the protection of a doorway. She slammed backward into the door, Cyrano still in her arms, and peeked out around the door frame.

The Nazi soldier looked up and down the street, and Samira ducked back behind the wall before he could see her. She waited a long, breathless moment, then peeked out again.

The Nazi soldier signaled to someone inside, and a woman staggered out into the street as though she had been pushed. She was followed by a young boy around Samira's age, and another woman carrying a baby, and an older man. Samira didn't recognize any of them, but her heart sank into her stomach at the thought that these might be the prisoners the Nazis had collected from the village last night.

And then, halfway back in the line of prisoners, Samira saw her mother. Kenza Zidane. She still wore a tan raincoat over her blue dress, and she held her back straight and her head up high. But Samira knew her mother. Knew she was tired, and afraid. Samira's heart stopped.

The last of the prisoners came out of the hotel, followed by a second Nazi soldier with a machine gun. He barked something at the prisoners, and together Samira's mother and the rest of them marched down the street, away from Samira.

Arms and legs shaking, Samira leaned back against the door and closed her eyes. *No. No no no no no.* The Nazis had abandoned Bayeux, but not their prisoners. They had left two soldiers behind to finish what they had started the night before, and now her mother and the other prisoners were being marched out of town, to be shot in the woods.

THE WASP'S STING

Samira trailed the prisoners and their Nazi guards through the streets of Bayeux. How could she stop the Nazi soldiers from shooting her mother and the other prisoners? She turned the problem over in her mind again and again. She had the knife the British glider soldier had given her. She had Cyrano too, and he was brave—braver than she was—but he was small. Samira had been the one to save *him* from the Nazis. Where was the French Resistance? Where were the Allied soldiers? The people of Bayeux? Was there no one who could help her?

The city gave way to fields and farmhouses, and Samira followed along behind a hedgerow, out of sight of the soldiers and the prisoners. She wished she could catch her mother's attention, let her know she was here, at least. But Kenza Zidane kept her eyes on the ground, just like the rest of the prisoners.

The soldiers steered the prisoners toward a small grove of trees, and Samira knew she was running out of time. She had to think of something. Had to *do* something.

I will attack them with my knife if I have to, Samira thought. It was suicide. She would be shot before she could do any real damage. But she would try. She was not going to let her mother and the others die without doing *something*.

It was harder to stay hidden in the woods. The trees were old, and tall, like giant pillars that held up a roof of green leaves, and there were wide-open spaces between them. Sunlight trickled down here and there, occasionally breaking through with a bright shaft, like a ray of light through a stained-glass window. The leaves formed a thin, soft, brown carpet that muffled Samira's footsteps. The tingle Samira got walking through the quiet, beautiful grove reminded her of the way she'd felt in the garden of the Grand Mosque in Paris.

But this magical place was about to be defiled by a horrible atrocity. Unless Samira could do something about it.

Samira waited until she thought she was out of sight of the guards and sprinted from the protection of one big tree to the next. She leaned back against the new tree, breathing heavily, but froze as she heard a familiar voice call out to her.

"No! Love of my life, you should not be here!" her mother cried.

Samira gasped. Her mother had seen her! She had called out to her in Arabic, guessing that the Nazis couldn't understand what she was saying. But had the guards seen her too? Samira couldn't peek around the tree for fear they would find her. Instead, she held her breath, listening for the sound of German boots, for her mother's voice.

"Run, Samira. Run far, far away from this place," her mother called in Arabic. "You should not be here to see this. And if they find you, they will kill you too. Run!"

One of the Nazis barked for Kenza Zidane to be quiet, and Samira heard her mother cry out in pain. Samira peeked out from behind the tree. One of the soldiers had struck Samira's mother in the back with the butt of his rifle, and she had staggered a few steps away, trying to stay on her feet. *No!* Samira's heart broke. Her mother had taken a chance calling out to her, had drawn attention to herself, and one of the wasps had stung her.

But they were planning to do far worse. The soldiers marched the prisoners to a clearing in the middle of the wood, where a half dozen old, dirty shovels rested against the trunk of a tree. Nearby, there were two freshly dug and re-covered plots of earth, each about five meters by five meters wide.

"Take the shovels and dig a hole as big as the others," one of the Nazis told the prisoners in French.

"Why?" asked one of the prisoners. A young boy.

"Just do as you're told," the Nazi said.

Samira felt like she was falling. Like she had stepped off the top of the Bayeux cathedral and was dropping like a stone. She swayed on her feet and had to put a hand out to brace herself, or she would have fallen for real.

The boy might not have understood what was happening, but Samira did.

The Nazis were making the prisoners dig their own grave before they shot them.

SAMIRA'S ARMY

Samira leaned against the tree at her back, her mind reeling. *Her mother was digging her own grave.* The horror of it threatened to swallow her whole. She had until her mother and the others were finished digging to figure something out, or this glade in the woods would be their final resting place.

And probably hers too.

Samira wiped the tears from her eyes, and as she blinked her focus back, she saw something strange at the bottom of a tree a few meters away.

It was a green helmet.

Samira frowned. What was a lone helmet doing all the way out here in the woods so far from anything? Slowly, dully, she put the pieces together. The Nazis wore gray helmets, not green. This one had a different shape from theirs too.

It was an Allied soldier's helmet.

Samira's heart leaped, but then reality set in. No Allied soldier was hiding anywhere nearby. He would have picked up his helmet and worn it. But where had it come from? And what had happened to the soldier? An idea, a recent memory, began to tickle the back of Samira's brain, and her eyes went up the tree trunk. Up, up, up— until she saw a parachute caught in the tree.

And dangling from it was another Rupert!

Butterflies flitted in Samira's chest as a plan began to form. She put Cyrano on the ground and whispered, "Stay. Stay here, Cyrano. Good dog." And without a moment's more hesitation, she ran for Rupert's tree.

The dummy wasn't making battle sounds, the way the other Rupert had been. Samira worried that meant it wasn't like the other one, that it did different things—or nothing at all. But Rupert was her last, best hope right now.

Samira grabbed a low branch and swung her legs up. Through the trees, she saw her mother, a shovel in her hand and already a foot lower in the ground, looking straight at Samira. Kenza Zidane's eyes were wide, and she shook her head once, quickly, so that Samira would see but the Nazis guards wouldn't.

Samira's mother didn't understand. And Samira had no time to explain.

A Nazi guard walked over and gestured for Samira's mother to get back to work. He turned to look in the direction that Samira's mother had been looking, but Samira was already gone, climbing up and around the backside of the tree. She wished she could comfort her mother. Let her know she had a plan. But Samira wasn't even sure it would work.

She just had to try.

Higher and higher Samira climbed, until she came face-to-face with the dummy. This one had RUPERT stenciled across his chest too, and she decided to call him Rupert Two.

"All right, Rupert Two," she whispered. "Why aren't you singing?"

Samira slid her hands over Rupert's jacket, being careful not to dislodge him from the tree—or activate anything explosive inside him. The end of a red wire peeked out from inside Rupert Two's collar, and Samira felt a little flicker of hope. Down below, the prisoners were still digging, but she didn't know how much time she had. She quickly unbuttoned Rupert's jacket, revealing a small black satchel on his chest. It was the thing that made the sound effects! Samira opened the satchel and saw a place inside where a wire could have been attached but wasn't.

If she connected the wire, would it play the battle sounds? Or would connecting the wire make Rupert Two explode? Samira was no engineer. All she knew was that there was a disconnected wire and a place where one could be attached. And she needed Rupert Two and his virtual army.

Samira held her breath and connected the wire.

Bang! KaBOOM! Rat-tat-tat-tat!

Rupert Two erupted in an explosion of sound, and Samira was so surprised she nearly lost her grip. Rupert Two hadn't exploded for *real* though. He was doing his other job—tricking the Nazis into thinking there was a battle raging nearby.

And it was working. Samira watched through the leaves as the Nazi soldiers and the prisoners all ducked, wondering where the fighting had come from all of a sudden. One of the soldiers barked for the prisoners to keep digging and stayed to guard them with the machine gun. The other guard, the one with the rifle, went off to investigate. The rifleman couldn't see Samira yet, and he sneaked from tree to tree as he went, afraid there was a real battle going on nearby.

It had worked! Samira grinned from ear to ear. She'd gotten one of the Nazi soldiers to leave the prisoners!

But then the smile left Samira's face. Rupert Two had done what he was supposed to do: lure one of the Nazi soldiers away. But that meant the Nazi soldier was coming right for Samira, trapped up here in a tree.

RUPERT TWO

Samira fumbled for the knife the British soldier had given her. It wasn't for the Nazi soldier. There was no way she could do anything to hurt the rifleman with her dagger.

The knife was for Rupert Two.

Samira attacked the strings connecting Rupert Two to his parachute. *Snip! Snip! Snip!* The British paratrooper, Clarke, had been right—the knife was sharp. It cut through the cords with ease. As each one was cut, Rupert Two twisted and jerked, dropping another few centimeters. The Nazi soldier was getting closer. Any second now, he would be right beneath the tree where Samira was hiding, where the crashing battle sound effects were still booming from inside the pouch under Rupert Two's uniform. The Nazi would look up, and he would see her there in the tree, would understand that there were no real Allied soldiers here, and he would take aim at her with his rifle and—

Snip! Samira cut another cord, and she jumped as Rupert Two shot down through the branches, his parachute whipping down through the tree behind him. The dummy tumbled as it fell, hitting branch after branch, and Samira held her breath, waiting for the explosion. The Nazi soldier looked up to see Rupert Two falling right toward him. The rifleman cried out and threw a hand up, but he was too slow to move out of the way. Rupert Two landed right on top of him, knocking him to the ground.

And nothing happened.

No explosion.

The Nazi and Rupert Two lay in a heap together, and the parachute fluttered down on top of them both. The battle sound effects weren't playing anymore—the wire must have come loose again in the fall, Samira thought. The rifleman kicked and cursed and tried to fight his way out from under the dummy and the parachute and the cords, but still Rupert Two didn't explode.

Any second now, the Nazi would be free.

Samira didn't know what to do. Climb down? Climb up? She had expected the dummy to explode. She had *needed* the dummy to explode. Instead, all she had done was kick the wasp's nest.

The Nazi soldier fought his way free of the parachute, and his eyes met Samira's. He glowered at her, angry at being tricked, mad at having a dummy and a parachute dropped on him, and he reached for his rifle. Still lying on his back, the German soldier lifted his weapon, found Samira in his rifle sights, and pulled the trigger.

THE END OF A RESCUE

Yip!

At the same moment the German soldier fired, Cyrano came flying in and clamped his tiny jaws around the man's wrist.

Pakow!

The rifleman's shot went wide, splintering a branch just to the right of Samira's head, and he cursed again. He struggled with the parachute cords and with Cyrano, trying to get to his feet. Off in the distance, Samira could see the rifleman's shot had gotten the attention of the second Nazi soldier, who was coming their way.

As a distraction, she and Cyrano and Rupert Two had done a bang-up job. But now what?

"Hang on, Cyrano!" Samira yelled. "I'm coming!"

The little dog growled and bit down harder, thrashing back and forth as the Nazi rifleman cried out in pain. He let go of his rifle and tried to pull Cyrano away.

Samira dropped from branch to branch as quickly as she dared. There was a long way to go. And what was she going to do when she got there? She had no idea. She still had the dagger, at least.

Just as she thought about the knife, and what she might have to do with it, Samira's foot slipped. She reached out in a panic for another branch to steady herself and caught it—but the knife went tumbling from her hands. She watched in horror as it bounced and caromed off branches all the way down, then skittered away on the forest floor, disappearing into the undergrowth.

Samira had no weapon now. No chance against two Nazi soldiers with guns.

Samira clambered down the rest of the way, her heart hammering in her chest. The last branch to the ground was a drop, and she landed feet-first but tumbled back on her bottom with an *oof*.

When she looked up, the second Nazi, the one with the machine gun, had run up and was standing right over her.

Samira closed her eyes and curled up into a ball, trembling.

WANG!

Samira felt a thump on the ground and opened her eyes.

The German soldier with the machine gun lay unconscious at her feet, and her mother, Kenza Zidane, stood over him with a shovel in both hands.

FROUFROU

Samira's mother tossed her shovel aside and picked up the machine gun the unconscious Nazi soldier had dropped. She swung it toward the rifleman, who was still struggling with Cyrano and the parachute.

"Enough," she said in French. "It's over."

The German soldier understood enough to stop struggling and put his hands up. Cyrano seemed to understand too, and he let go of the soldier's wrist and backed away, still growling, still watchful. Samira's mother picked up the Nazi's rifle and slung it over her shoulder.

Samira stood and flew at her mother, wrapping her in a hug.

"Maman!" Samira cried.

"Love of my life," Samira's mother said. She hugged Samira back as best she could while still aiming the machine gun at the soldier. "You did a foolish thing, coming here when I told you not to," she said. "But a brave one too," she added, and Samira's heart soared. Foolish or not, brave or not, it had worked, and that's all that really mattered to Samira. Her mother was safe!

And so were the other prisoners. They came up behind Kenza Zidane, mothers and grandparents hugging their young ones, many of them crying. They all knew now how close they had come to dying, and the relief in their faces was heartbreaking.

Samira waved her mother and the others back. "Be careful—the dummies on the parachutes, they explode!" Samira said.

The German soldier who'd been struggling with the parachute understood enough French to freeze, suddenly horrified by the burlap dummy he lay beside. Samira's mother and the others moved back, leaving him alone with the explosive.

"Get yourself out of there," Kenza told the German soldier. "When he's free," she told the others, "if he doesn't blow up, tie him to the tree."

"You're not going to kill him?" one of the old men among the prisoners said. "They were about to shoot us and bury us in a mass grave!"

"And if we kill him now, we'd be no better," Samira's mother said. "We'll leave him for the Allied soldiers. The invasion began this morning."

"It's true! They've been parachuting in and coming in on gliders all night," Samira said. "That's why all the German soldiers left Bayeux. They're running away!"

That caused a flurry of conversation among the prisoners.

"Move," Samira's mother told the Nazi soldier.

Very slowly, very carefully, the German rifleman slid out from under the parachute and away from Rupert Two. The dummy didn't explode, and when the rifleman was clear, some of the women tied him and the unconscious German soldier to the tree with belts and bootlaces.

Cyrano yipped excitedly, making Samira scared that some other Nazi soldier had found them. But his tail wagged furiously and he barked happily as he tore through the crowd, into the outstretched arms of a little girl half Samira's age.

"Froufrou!" she cried, and the tiny dog licked her face all over.

Froufrou? Samira had given the dog the name Cyrano because she didn't know what his real name was, and over the last few hours he'd *become* Cyrano for her. But his real name was Froufrou, apparently, and he too had rescued his family. Samira felt a tinge of sadness at his sudden abandonment, but she understood. The girl and her mother were his real family. Cyrano and Samira had just been temporary Allies with a common goal.

"What do we do now?" one of the woman prisoners asked.

"If the Nazis really have abandoned Bayeux, it's probably safest to go back there. For now," Samira's mother said, and everyone agreed. Samira's mother kept the machine gun for herself and gave the rifle to one of the old men, and together they began the tired, wary walk back to the city. Along the way, Samira held her mother's hand tight. She wasn't sure she was ever going to let go again.

Her mother squeezed her hand, and Samira laid her head against her mother's side.

"I didn't think I would be able to save you," Samira told her mother. "Everywhere I went, I met people who could help. But they all said no. The French Resistance, the Allied soldiers, the people of Bayeux. No one would help me."

"But they did," Samira's mother said. "No one of them saved us, but each of them, in their own way, they did the jobs they were supposed to do, which allowed you to do your job: rescue me and all these people. You're a hero, Samira Zidane, and I'm proud of you."

Samira glowed.

As they walked, Samira felt a playful nip at her heels. It was Cyrano! Saying hello to let her know he hadn't forgotten her.

"You are a very good dog, Cyrano," Samira told him. She still couldn't bring herself to call him Froufrou.

"What do *we* do now?" Samira asked her mother.

For the past three years, she and her mother had worked for the French Resistance. But now it seemed like the war was over.

"There is still much work to be done, love of my life," Samira's mom said. "The war isn't finished. Not by a long way. If the invasion is successful, and I pray that it is, we here in Normandy may soon be safe. But there is still the rest of France and all of Europe and our homeland in Algeria and many other places left to be freed. We will continue to resist when we need to."

Samira nodded. "And what about today?" she asked.

Her mother smiled. "Today, we will welcome our liberators into Bayeux, and help them where and how we can. And then, Samira, I believe we have earned ourselves a good night's sleep."

To read more about Samira,
pick up Alan Gratz's new novel, *Allies*!

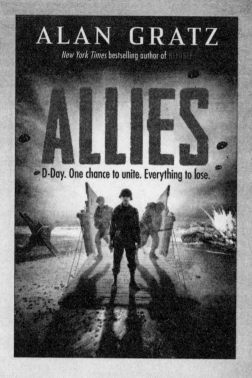

Welcome to D-Day: The biggest, most top-secret operation ever, with the Allied nations coming together—by land, sea, and air—to storm German-occupied France. Dee, a young U.S. soldier, is on a boat racing toward the French coast. Behind enemy lines in France, a girl named Samira works as a spy, trying to sabotage the German army. Meanwhile, paratrooper James leaps from a plane to join a daring raid. And Henry, a medic, goes out into the bullets and bombs, searching for soldiers to save. But with betrayals and deadly risks at every turn, can the Allies do what it takes to win?

Heart-pounding action. High-stakes danger.
Books you can't put down.

When two soldiers from different sides collide during the Battle of Okinawa, the decisions they make will change *everything*.

Three different kids. Three different time periods. One mission in common: escape. The bestselling modern classic!

In Nazi Germany, a boy named Michael joins the Hitler Youth . . . but as a spy. Can he take down the enemy from within?

Ten concentration camps. It's something no one could imagine surviving. But it is what Yanek Gruener has to face. Based on an incredible true story.

With his life on the line, can Kamran clear his brother's name by unlocking a series of secret codes?

ABOUT THE AUTHOR

Photo credit: Wes Stitt

ALAN GRATZ is the *New York Times* bestselling author of several acclaimed books for young readers, including *Refugee*, a *New York Times* Notable Book and an Amazon, *Kirkus Reviews*, and *Publishers Weekly* Best Book of the Year; *Grenade*, the 2018 Freeman Book Award winner; *Projekt 1065*, a *Kirkus Reviews* Best Book of the Year; *Prisoner B-3087*, winner of eight state awards and included on YALSA's 2014 Best Fiction for Young Adults list; and *Code of Honor*, a YALSA 2016 Quick Pick for Reluctant Young Adult Readers. Alan lives in North Carolina with his wife and daughter. Look for him online at alangratz.com.